SLITHERING SNAKES

Copperheads

BLASTOFF! READERS 2

by Suzane Nguyen

BELLWETHER MEDIA • MINNEAPOLIS, MN

Blastoff! Readers are carefully developed by literacy experts to build reading stamina and move students toward fluency by combining standards-based content with developmentally appropriate text.

Level 1 provides the most support through repetition of high-frequency words, light text, predictable sentence patterns, and strong visual support.

Level 2 offers early readers a bit more challenge through varied sentences, increased text load, and text-supportive special features.

Level 3 advances early-fluent readers toward fluency through increased text load, less reliance on photos, advancing concepts, longer sentences, and more complex special features.

★ **Blastoff! Universe**

This edition first published in 2025 by Bellwether Media, Inc.

Library of Congress Cataloging-in-Publication Data

Names: Nguyen, Suzane, author.
Title: Copperheads / by Suzane Nguyen.
Description: Minneapolis, MN : Bellwether Media, Inc., 2025. | Series: Blastoff! readers: slithering snakes | Includes bibliographical references and index. | Audience: Ages 5-8 | Audience: Grades K-1 | Summary: "Simple text and full-color photography introduce beginning readers to copperheads. Developed by literacy experts for students in kindergarten through third grade"-- Provided by publisher.
Identifiers: LCCN 2024003099 (print) | LCCN 2024003100 (ebook) | ISBN 9798886870374 (library binding) | ISBN 9781644878811 (ebook)
Subjects: LCSH: Copperhead--Juvenile literature.
Classification: LCC QL666.O69 N48 2025 (print) | LCC QL666.O69 (ebook) | DDC 597.96/3--dc23/eng/20240208
LC record available at https://lccn.loc.gov/2024003099
LC ebook record available at https://lccn.loc.gov/2024003100

Editor: Betsy Rathburn Designer: Brittany McIntosh

Printed in the United States of America, North Mankato, MN.

Table of Contents

Venom and Fangs 4
Ambush Attackers 10
Yellow Tails 18
Glossary 22
To Learn More 23
Index 24

Venom and Fangs

Copperheads are dangerous snakes. They have a **venomous** bite!

They are common in the eastern and central United States.

Copperhead Range

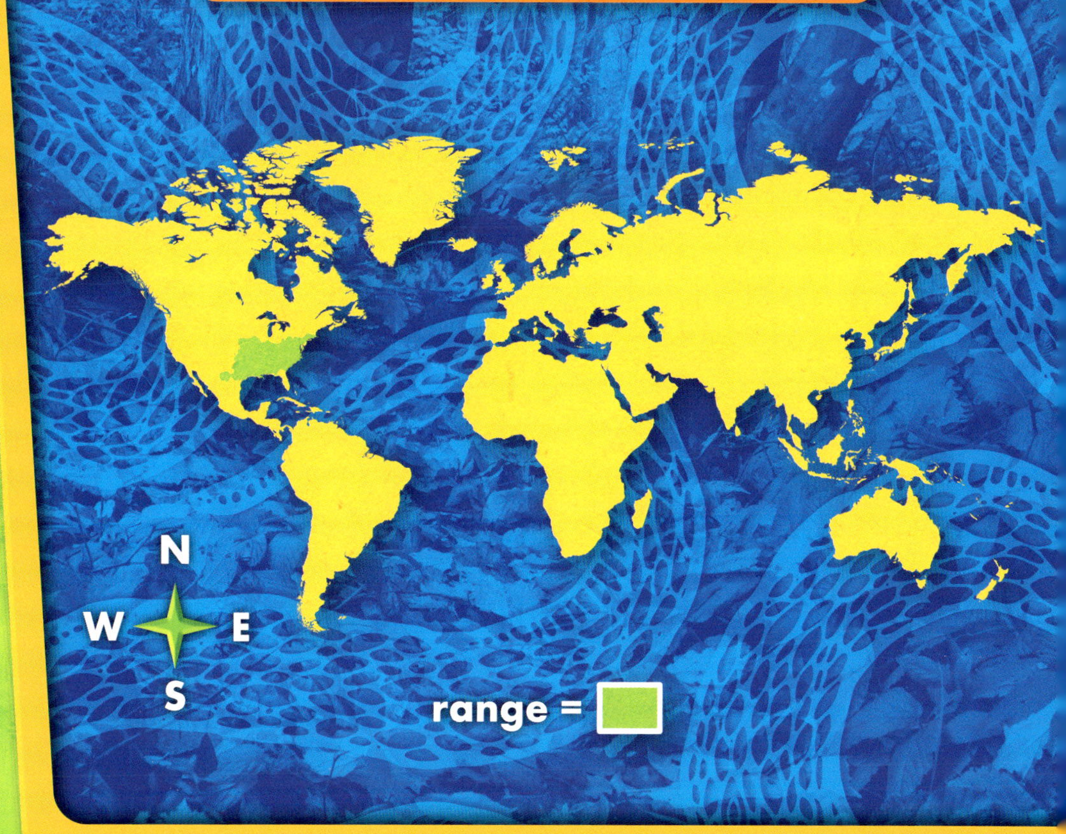

Copperheads usually have brown **scales**. They have dark hourglass-shaped markings.

They have **pit organs** near their eyes. Long **fangs** help them catch meals.

Spot a Copperhead!

Copperheads grow up to 3 feet (0.9 meters) long. Males are longer than females.

Size Comparison

baseball bat: up to 2.8 feet (0.8 meters) long

copperhead: up to 3 feet (0.9 meters) long

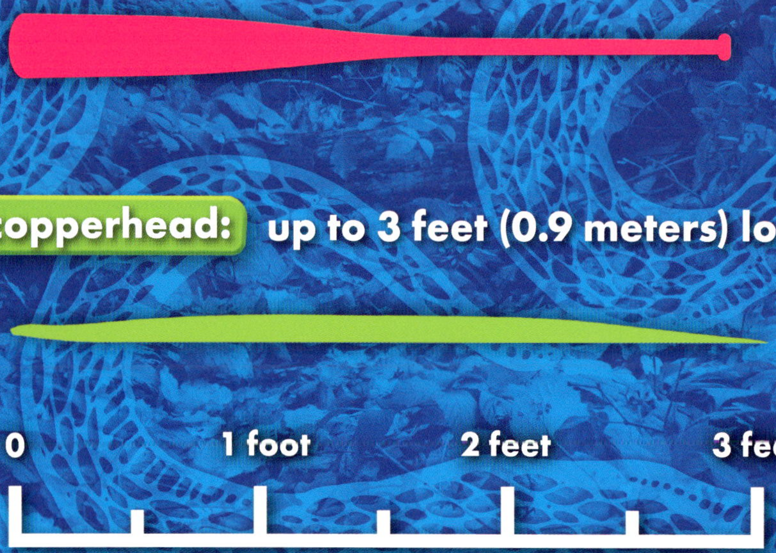

The snakes usually weigh less than 1 pound (0.5 kilograms).

Ambush Attackers

Copperheads live in **wetlands** and rocky hillsides.

They often hide in trees and bushes. Sometimes they swim in ponds or rivers.

Copperheads are **ambush** hunters. Their pit organs help them find heat from **prey**.

When prey is near, copperheads bite! Their fangs let out deadly venom.

These snakes
are **carnivores**.
They eat toads, lizards,
and mice.

One meal can keep them
full for weeks!

Copperhead Food

Copperheads **bask** on warm days. They **hibernate** in winter. They rest among rocks.

Coyotes and owls hunt copperheads. Copperheads hide to stay safe.

Yellow Tails

Female copperheads give birth to live young. They can have over 20 babies at once.

Copperheads are born with yellow tails. This lasts three or four years.

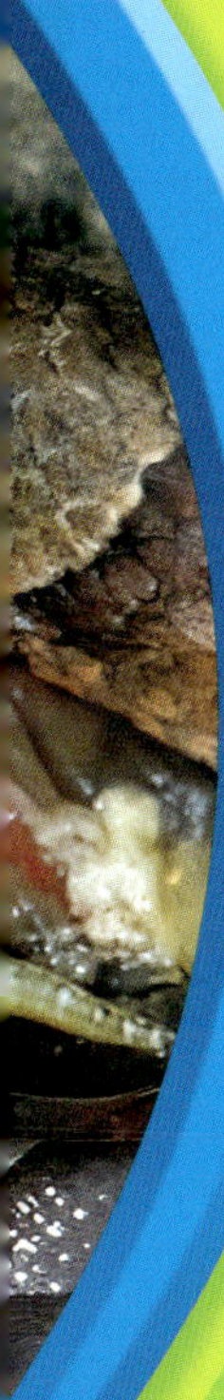

The snakes can hunt right after birth.

They are fully grown after about four years. Then they have their own babies!

Copperhead Stats

status in the wild: least concern

life span: up to 18 years

Glossary

ambush—related to hunting by lying in wait

bask—to lay in the sun; cold-blooded animals often bask to raise their body temperatures.

carnivores—animals that only eat meat

fangs—long, sharp teeth

hibernate—to pass the winter by sleeping or resting

pit organs—body parts that help snakes sense heat

prey—animals that are hunted by other animals for food

scales—plates that cover an animal's body

venomous—able to produce venom; venom is a kind of poison made by some snakes.

wetlands—areas of land that are covered with low levels of water for most of the year

To Learn More

AT THE LIBRARY

Feldman, Thea. *Snakes Smell with Their Tongues!: And Other Amazing Facts.* New York, N.Y.: Simon Spotlight, 2021.

Hicks, Kelli. *Copperheads.* New York, N.Y.: Crabtree Publishing, 2022.

Thielges, Alissa. *Curious About Snakes.* Mankato, Minn.: Amicus, 2023.

ON THE WEB

FACTSURFER

Factsurfer.com gives you a safe, fun way to find more information.

1. Go to www.factsurfer.com.

2. Enter "copperheads" into the search box and click .

3. Select your book cover to see a list of related content.

Index

ambush, 12
babies, 18, 20
bask, 16
bite, 4, 13
bushes, 11
carnivores, 14
colors, 6, 7, 19
coyotes, 17
fangs, 7, 13
females, 8, 18
food, 14, 15
hibernate, 16
hide, 11, 17
hillsides, 10
hunt, 12, 17, 20
males, 8
markings, 6, 7
owls, 17
pit organs, 6, 7, 12
ponds, 11
prey, 12, 13
range, 5
rivers, 11
scales, 6, 7
size, 8, 9
stats, 21
swim, 11
tails, 19
trees, 11
United States, 5
venom, 4, 13
wetlands, 10
winter, 16

The images in this book are reproduced through the courtesy of: Dennis W Donohue, front cover; fivespots, pp. 3, 7; CBBB/ Alamy, p. 4; jadimages, p. 6; Kushan Nirmal 369, p. 7 (inset); Matthew L Niemiller, p. 9; Andrew DuBois/ Alamy, p. 10; Scott Buckel/ Alamy, p. 11; Jay Ondreicka, p. 12; Suzanna Ruby, p. 13; Norman Owen Tomalin/ Alamy, p. 14; Auscape International Pty Ltd/ Alamy, pp. 14-15; All Canada Photos/ Alamy, p. 15 (toads); Ryan M. Bolton, p. 15 (lizards); jitkagold, p. 15 (mice); Creeping Things, p. 16; NajaShots, p. 17; E.R. Degginger/ Alamy, p. 18; Robert Hamilton/ Alamy, p. 19; Breck P. Kent, p. 20; Wirestock, pp. 20-21; Eric Isselee, p. 23.